TAARA OF THE STARS

Book 1

Enter the ZyGniC!

hachette INDIA

ZyGniC ENTERTAINMENT

TAARA OF THE STARS

Book 1

Enter the ZyGniC!

'Enter the ZyGniC!' is the first book in a five-book series from Indian entertainment start-up Zygnic Entertainment.

'Taara of the Stars' is the first series set within the Zygnian Multiverse.

Zygnic Entertainment is a niche creator-owned studio that develops and creates original IP.

. . .

www.taaraofthestars.com

Team Zygnic

Praveen Balakrishnan
WRITER

ROSH
ART DIRECTOR

Abhilash Narayanan
ILLUSTRATOR

Sharath Raj
COLOURS

Lucas Gattoni
LETTERS

Shyamnath
INKS

Binyas and Arya
COLOUR FLATS

Sunil Bhaskaran
DIGITAL MARKETING

Nayana Praveen
ADMINISTRATION

First published in 2023 by Hachette India
(Registered name:
Hachette Book Publishing India Pvt. Ltd)
An Hachette UK company
www.hachetteindia.com
1

Reprint specifications may be subject to change including but not limited to finishes, paper, text colour and colour sections.

ISBN: 978-93-93701-63-3

For sale in the Indian Subcontinent only

Hachette Book Publishing India Pvt. Ltd
4th & 5th Floors, Corporate Centre
Plot No. 94, Sector 44, Gurugram – 122003, India

Created, designed and typeset by
Zygnic Entertainment

Printed and bound in India by
Manipal Technologies Limited

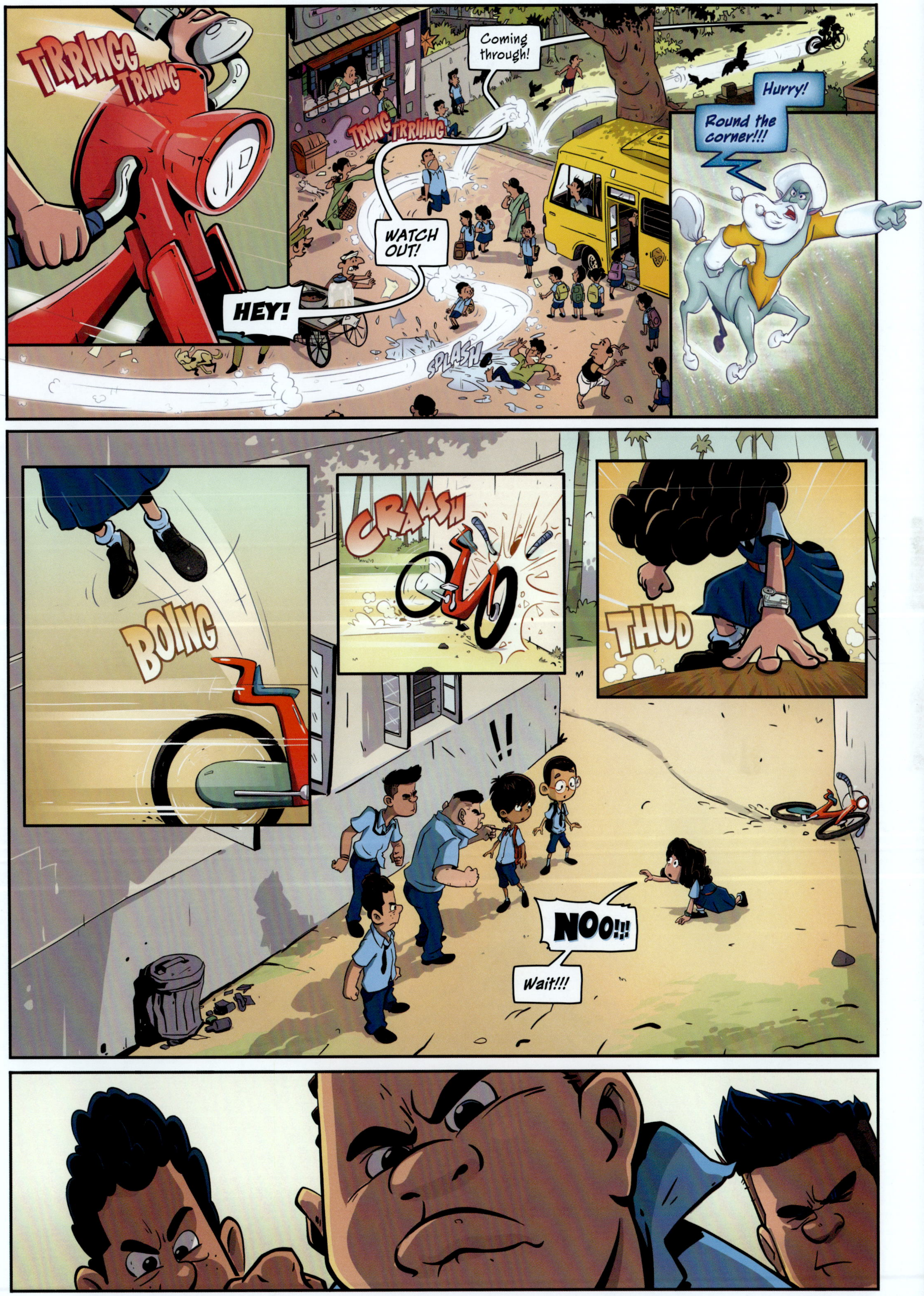
TRRINGG TRINNG
TRING TRRIING
Coming through!
WATCH OUT!
HEY!
SPLASH
Hurry!
Round the corner!!!
BOING
CRAASH
THUD
!!
NOO!!!
Wait!!!

A FEW HOURS AGO...
Aakash, Rehan, c'mon, guys...
What do you mean I'll have to let them go?
Buddy, understand this...
HALF PRICE SALE
...It's not the dragons you are buying...
Or the bottles!
Instead, what you get...
...is the opportunity to set them free...all that for 20 bucks!
Freedom. Of the dragons, for the dragons...by you!
FREEDOM SOOPER CHEAP
Ask not what your money can do for you...
...but what you can do for the dragonflies!
C'mon, man! Just take the money and gimme that.
NOPE! It's the principle of the thing.
DUMMIES!
You hear that, Rehan?
Today's kids... no morals!
I mean...who wouldn't want to buy some freedom?
From the looks of it... Everyone.
Aakash, we didn't sell a single bottle!
This isn't working.
Let's wrap up.

I release you...fly high, my friends.
Live long and prosper.
That felt good.
You DO realise, don't you, that it was us...You and I... who trapped and bottled those flies?
Well...you never appreciate something unless you lose it... at least once!
I bet those dragonflies are a whole lot happier now!!!
We are still broke. Flat broke...
sigh And in debt...I know.
Ahah! Look who's here.
If it isn't dumb and dumber!
You better have our money.
Please...
No...no...
TRING TRRIIING
CRAASH
THUD
NOO!!!
Wait!!!

AND SO...
Look...I **really** don't want to hurt you.
tap tap tap
Ish that sho little babykins...
SWUP
I'm sho sho shcaaared...
TAP
POW!
GLARG!
!
Uuuuuhhh...
BADAHM
UHRRR!!!
DISH KYOOM
SPLAT
DISHOOM!
PHUFF
AAAH!
SLAP SLAP SLAP
You seeing this?
Yup.
Did she just...
Yup.
What happens to us?
The usual. Probably worse...
Yup.

You think she's finished?
They are...
They should be running...
You guys should probably leave.
That way.
SHE'S NOT WITH US!
WE DON'T KNOW...
...her.
HIHAHIHO HOHO
That's...that!
Hi, guys... wonderful seeing you!
I'm Taara.
I'd love to stay and talk...but it's getting late.
Catch up tomorrow then.
Bye-aye.
Who was *that?*
?
What did she mean "catch up tomorrow"?
!?!
THE NEXT DAY...
"Bro..."
"Yup?"
SHIKSHA HIGH SCHOOL

The girl from yesterday...
Uh-hunh.
Today is tomorrow...
I know.
Bullies out to get us...
Undone homework...
And now this...
A girl.
Life...
...it's kind of complicated, bro.
Oh it sure is! Very, very complicated!
SKRRRT
AIYEE!
How...
...did you...
...just pop in?
Hi...
Hi...
We really must get to know each other better...
...considering that we are best friends...
What???
Hi, Taara...
...and classmates...
What???
Hi, Taara...
TIME TABLE
...we really, really must get to know each other better!
Morning, Taara!
Hi, Taara.
Heyyy, Taara...
Taara!!!

How...howww does everyone know her?
Tsk-tsk boys! Stop fighting!!
Taara, get the class in order...
She is the monitor?
!
Huh? Don't ask ME!
As the mystery deepens further...
MATHS
Z
...Aakash learns the meaning of Zzzzzzero.
Z Z Z Z Z
TTRRRIIIIINGGGGGG
Take a break, children...
...after you solve the problem on the board!
Hey...
....
It's a crisis – this is no time for maths!
PAFF!
Hey!!!

She wasn't here yesterday. I have never seen her before. And now, **today,** everyone knows her?
It's like she's been here the whole term.
I don't get it, man. It's driving me nuts.
THUD
This is beyond weird.
Life...my friend...
...is really, **incredibly** complicated!
Uh-huh.
Wonder where's she rushing off to now?
All clear.
ZyGniC...!
Hey...wake up!
ZZWUP
Greetings, Zwullian.
Is it him?
It's **possible.** The medallion...
What medallion?
Who is that?
Behind you...

Greetings, young ones!
!
I am Zzzg...
SNAP!
ZWUP!
!?!
Umm...we need to talk, right?
Who are you?
Who's that horseman?
What is this?
WHAT IS HAPPENING?
TRRRRIINGG
TRRRIIIIINGGGGGG
There goes the bell...
TRRRRRIIIIIIIINNNNGGGGG
Hey, you said "talk".
I didn't say when.

HEYY!
You cant just walk o...
...off.
She just did.
Something tells me this is going to happen a lot.
As the unusual day winds to a close...
TRRRRIINGG
SCHOOL
See you tomorrow, children.
ZzzZzz...
Taara...hey...
WAIT!
YAAAAWWNN
C'mon, guys... everyone's already gone.
ZHUMM!
My apologies, young ones...
Zyggy!!!
WHA...?
The ship!
You need to get to it now!!!

GO ZyGniC!!!
Is that a horse? Or a man? And what in the world's a ZyGniC!?
I don't know...what do we do now?
We follow the lady.
Quick, come on!
SCREECHHH
MY CYCLE!
Look. The chain...
It's broken. Someone has taken my bicycle.
Look, footsteps.
These are size 9 shoes.
It's those tough guys. This is their doing.
You sure?
What is your problem with them anyway?
It's a long story...
It all began with Tic/Toc.
Tick tock? As in a clock?
Oh no...that's their nickname.

Biren and Bidya. Identical twins.
They are eighth graders.
They know everyone who is someone...loads of connections.
They've got a neat little trading operation...
You need something... anything...they've got it...
...for a price of course.
Everything's business...the whole world's a trade.
They sound cool!
Hrrmph! They look cool, but that's about it.
Actually quite nasty... if you ask me.
Okay...go on...what happened next?
Him! It's all his fault.
Him and his science projects.
Ahah!!! And what about your "dragon"?
DRAGON?
I'll explain. We were looking for the slowest snail in the world. Thing is, I was trying to understand...
...the fluency of motion within the framework of time.
What... what... what?
Just stuff that fills Rehan's head. You should see his grades!
Shhh...maybe I should tell this story. So, Rehan needs a snail...and I go to Tic/Toc. They say they have it...but...
Mmph...

"...but they needed something in return.
"So I gave them a seven-headed dragon made in invisible ink."
A what???
Nothing. The paper was blank... no dragon...
He was just making stuff up.
NO I WASN'T!!! You don't know that.
Come on, man! But Tic/Toc were better...that world's slowest snail, they gave him, in return...
"...was actually dead!!!
"But things got bad when the twins sold the dragon paper to Scoot Junior for 20 bucks...
"...who also bought the snail from us for another 20 bucks..."
Hold on...wait a minute. If you guys knew it was dead, then why'd you sell it?
Umm...well, it was the world's slowest snail after all.
Maybe...it was just very slow...very very slow...
...could be, you know?
Aww, come on, be honest! We knew it was dead...but we were broke and well, Tic/Toc did it to us, first...so...
"Anyway...Scoot Junior ended up burning the paper, while trying to activate the invisible ink.
"And soon discovered that...ummmm...the snail was...let's just say... very, very slow..."

"So off he goes... running, to Scoot Senior, the biggest, meanest, bully in the school...
"...who goes to Tic/Toc, who promptly direct him to Aakash...
"...well, let's just say... Scoot convinced Aakash that the snail was dead and the paper...was blank!
"And...Aakash gave him the 40 and agreed to pay up 100 more.
But wait...you guys only got 40 bucks, right?
"Well, Scoot said we owed him "collection charges" and...umm...well... we were in no position to bargain, so...
I thought our "Freedom for Dragonflies" start-up would bring in some cash, but NO, probably cause of the...the...
Recession?
Yeah, that... and all.
Sigh Anyway, we couldn't pay them, they came looking for us, you popped in, and...here we are!
So, you two aren't exactly innocent! If I'd known that earlier, I wouldn't have rushed into that fight.
Anyway, I need to find my bicycle.
Look, I'm not too sure about her...we don't know who she is...
...or where she is from, or what she's up to.
You guys coming or what?
Look, talk to Grandma, all right? She usually has answers.
Yeah...

TAARA!
JUST WAIT FOR US... OKAY?
BE BACK IN A SEC...
HEY...
Let's get to the library. There's a phone there.
C'mon.
TRING... TRING...
TR TICK
Hi, Grandma.
Aakash. Something's wrong, isn't it?
Howw...
Grannies always know, kiddo.
Go on...
It's a long story, Grandma... ummm...well, it all started with a snail...
And Aakash tells Grandma...everything!
Then Tic/Toc...
...and Scoot said...
I thought we could pay up and be done with it, but the dragonfly start-up tanked cause of the...the... procession and all, and...
What???
Forget that... If Taara hadn't shown up when she did, things would've been really bad for us, Grandma.
She stood up for us, Grandma. And now she's in trouble.
I must help her out. It's the least I can do.
Uh oh.
Okay, take a deep breath and listen carefully. First off, you shouldn't have tricked those boys...they were right to be upset.

But...
Aakash... listen.
Secondly, no matter **what,** you won't go dealing with them on your own. The boys are way bigger and older than you.
You will be putting yourselves at risk – and her too.
Okay...
Now, I know that you think it's important to stand up for your friend who helped you.
It is. But not in a situation where all of you get into **more** trouble.
Violence is never **ever** an answer to anything.
Don't put yourselves in an impossible situation.
There is nothing wrong or weak in backing out of something you don't fully understand.
Or getting your near ones to help, when you need them.
And thirdly, I'm calling Aman to meet up with you guys.
He's older, more experienced and the boys will listen to him.
So, when he comes there, **that's** when you go...got it?
Oh dear...this boy is always in a hurry.
What now?
The truth, Rehan. We need to know what's going on.
KTING
By the way...I didn't understand why the dragonflies went on a procession?
What?
You said...
Recession... I said rece...
Aww, **shut up**...that isn't what you said!
Taara, look, you need to tell us... and right now...whatever's going on.
Yeah, me too. You can't keep hiding...things!
Either that or count me out!
What things?
WHOOSH
Taara, hurry!
FWEEET!
THESE THINGS!
Guys...there isn't time. You **have** to trust me... Please! I'll tell you everything, I promise, but if we don't get that cycle...and **really** quickly, something **terribly bad** is going to happen.

No, no, no, this isn't right....I can't. Grandma told us to wait for Aman.
ZyGniC!
NO!
snap
Wait...wait. Let's try to work out where the bike is and then decide what to do.
Why can't he tell us where it is?
He isn't a magician. He needs data, and right now, there isn't any.
Tic/Toc would know...they always know.
Point. Trouble is, we need to give them something in exchange.
Do you have a white sheet of paper?
The invisible ink stunt? Again? It won't work, again!
You know I could just zap them, right???
No, you won't. No violence, Taara. I've got this covered.
Might work...it's the repression and all...
Man! Rece...aww, forget it.
Aren't we overreacting? It's just a cycle after all...
No, it isn't...
And soon enough...Tic/Toc's lair: The cafeteria.
CAFE
I want some information on a stolen bike.
Hmmm...it all depends...
What you got to trade for it?
slurrrrrp
How about THE SMALLEST drawing ever made?
So small you can't even see it?
Best thing to own in a...umm... suppression.
In a what?
The invisible ink stunt? You are pulling that...again?
HAHAHAHAHAHAHAHAHA
Recession, Aakash... recession!

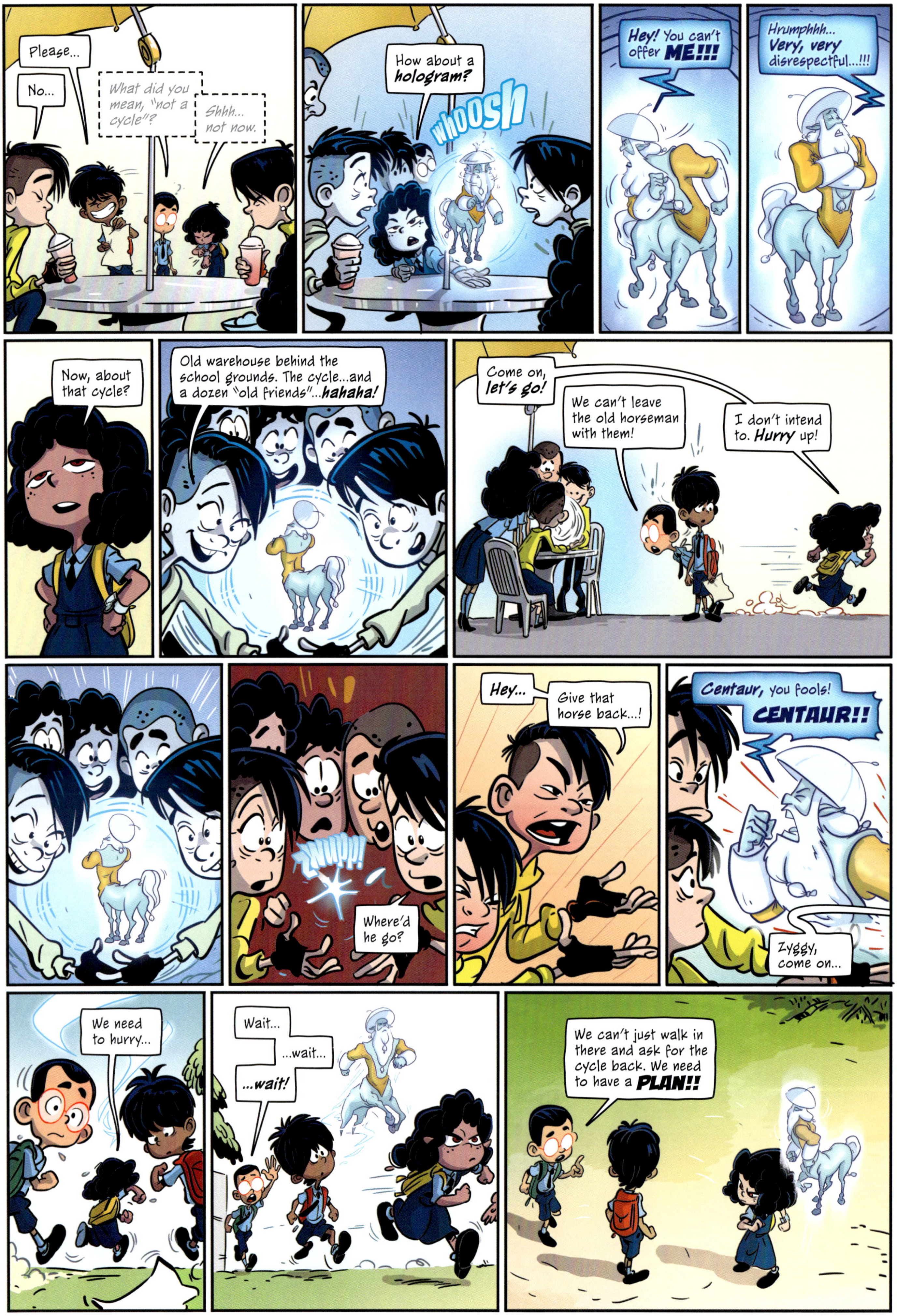
Please...
No...
What did you mean, "not a cycle"?
Shhh... not now.
How about a hologram?
WHOOSH
Hey! You can't offer ME!!!
Hrumphhh... Very, very disrespectful...!!!
Now, about that cycle?
Old warehouse behind the school grounds. The cycle...and a dozen "old friends"...hahaha!
Come on, let's go!
We can't leave the old horseman with them!
I don't intend to. Hurry up!
ZWUPP!
Where'd he go?
Hey...
Give that horse back...!
Centaur, you fools! CENTAUR!!
Zyggy, come on...
We need to hurry...
Wait...
...wait...
...wait!
We can't just walk in there and ask for the cycle back. We need to have a PLAN!!

And...Grandma has asked us to wait for Aman.
I HAVE A PLAN, MY RIGHT FIST...!
Temper, temper...
Taara, the boy is right.
You do need a plan.
So, what do we do?
The question is what can you do? The best plan is one that plays to your strengths. What are you good at?
Hah! Dental adjustment...!
I'm good at...wait a minute! Aren't we complicating things? It's just a cycle, isn't it? What'll they do? Eat it?
Maybe they'll bang it some, bust the lights, puncture a tyre...what more?
They've probably done that anyway.
If they dump it somewhere, Mr. Four Legs here could track it, right?
She said it isn't just a cycle.
So what is it?
It's a Model Z temporal engine with a bosonic core and a warp ratio of 1:21.
There's a damaged auto-destruct flip that seems to have been activated...
You didn't understand a thing, did you?
Man...I still don't know what a "riskassion" is, and you expect me to know all that?
Aww, come on, we need to get to the ship before the countdown ends.
Countdown to what?
KABOOM! The biggest kaboom ever...
And soon enough!
But why would a cycle go kaboom?
So, what is it?
It isn't just a cycle.
It's a Model Z tempor....
Shhh...Shut up guys. Look it's open...
Wait...let's wait for Aman.

Stay low...
They're in there.
KTIN!
AIEEEE!!!
YOU BRUTE!
WBUM
DISHOOM!!
AIEE!
DHUM
AIEE!
WHOOSH!!
DHUD
DHUD
SPLAT
UFF
DISHOOM
Well...that decides it.
Grab the bike.
Taara! There's a display here, and...
IT'S COUNTING DOWN!!!
00:00:30 ET
TAARAAA!!!
Something's about to happen!
00:00:28
PISKYU
No, no, no, no....

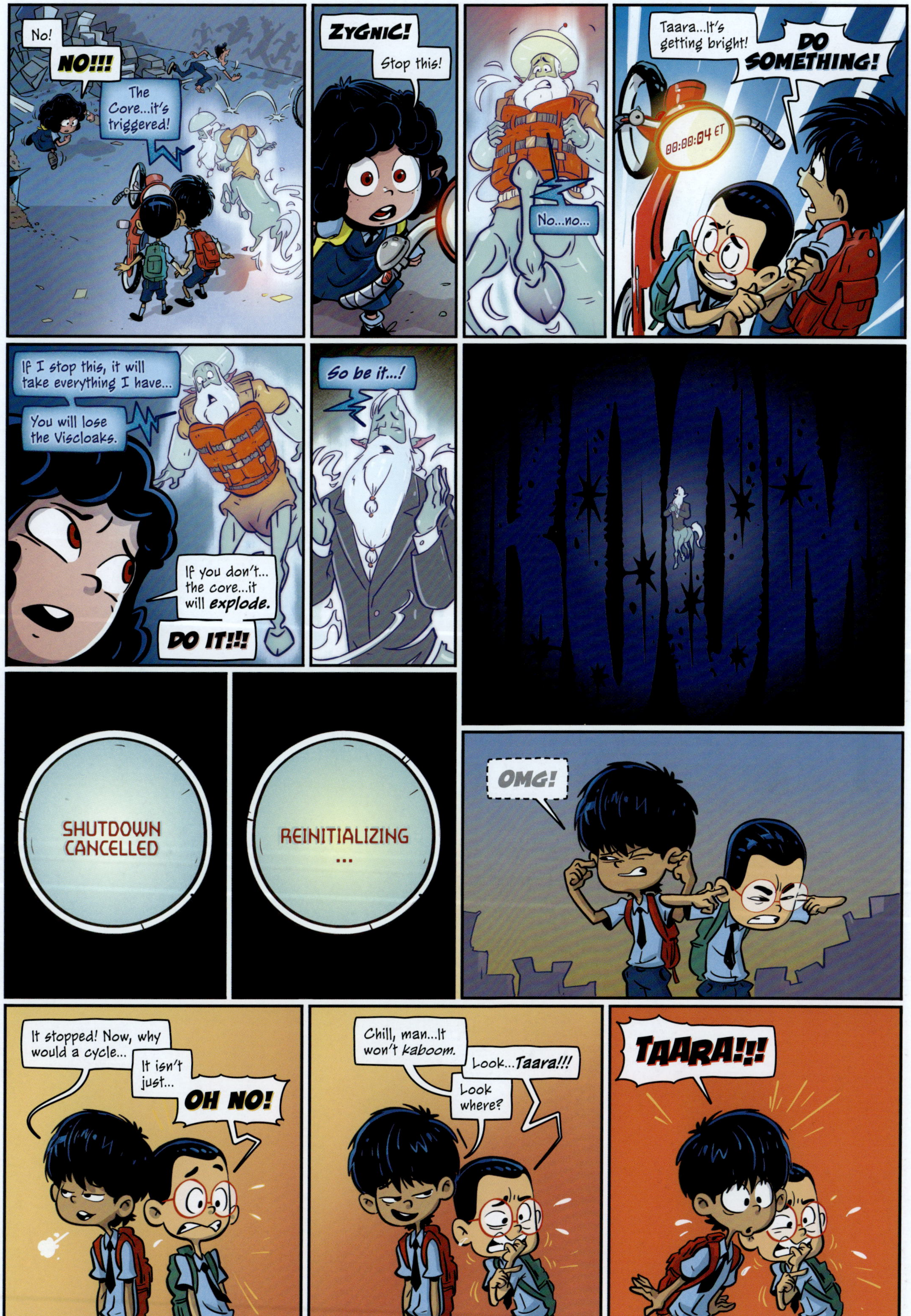
No!
NO!!!
The Core...it's triggered!
ZYGNIC!
Stop this!
No...no...
Taara...It's getting bright!
DO SOMETHING!
00:00:04 ET
If I stop this, it will take everything I have...
You will lose the Viscloaks.
If you don't... the core...it will explode.
DO IT!!!
So be it...!
BOOM
SHUTDOWN CANCELLED
REINITIALIZING ...
OMG!
It stopped! Now, why would a cycle...
It isn't just...
OH NO!
Chill, man...It won't kaboom.
Look...Taara!!!
Look where?
TAARA!!!

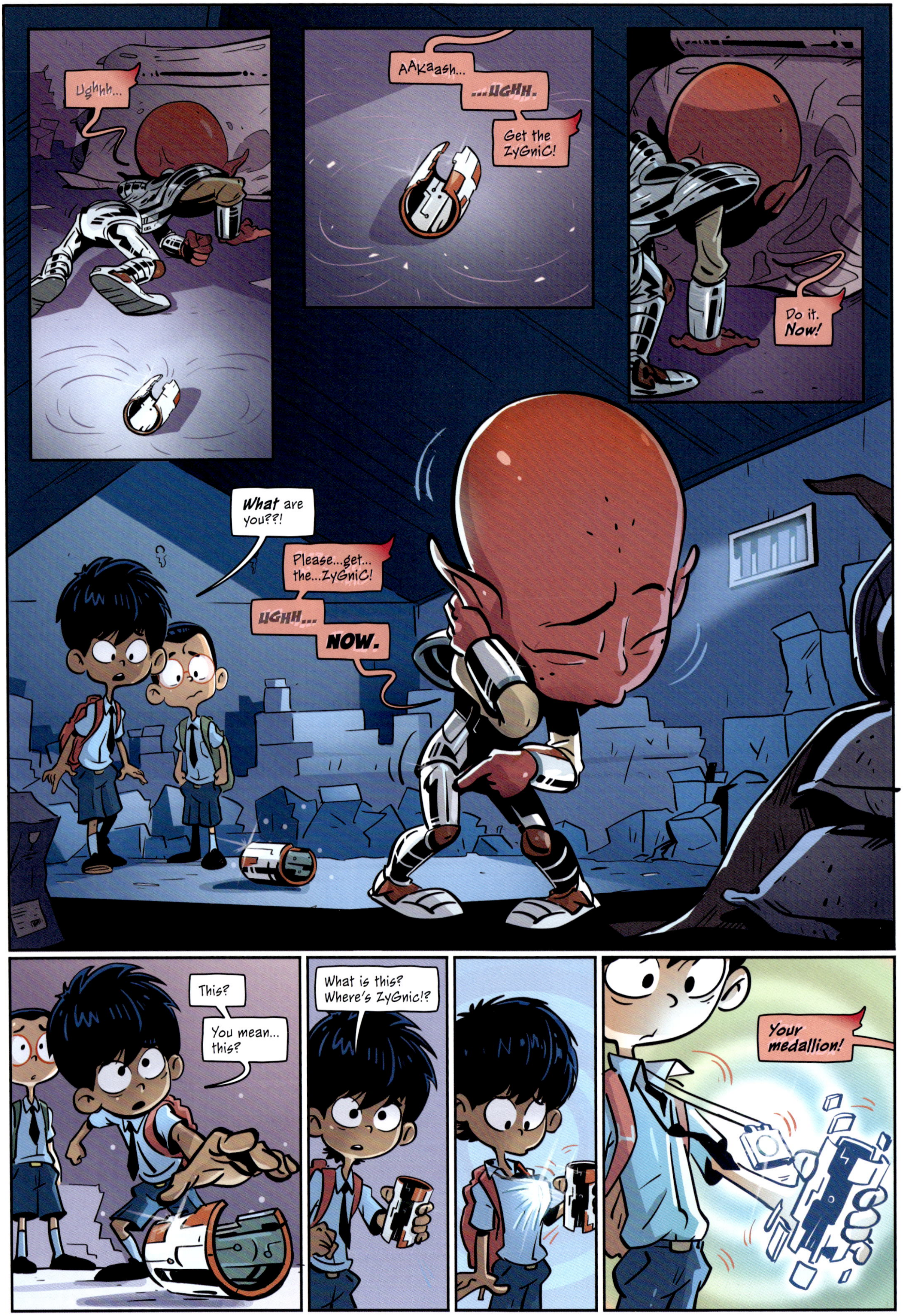
Ughhh...
AAkaash...
...UGHH.
Get the ZyGniC!
Do it. Now!
What are you??!
Please...get... the...ZyGniC!
UGHH...
NOW.
This?
You mean... this?
What is this? Where's ZyGnic!?
Your medallion!

!?!
Wha...What's happening?
Release the medallion...
SNAP
WOAHHH!
STRICK...
TICK...
KTRIICK!
CLICK
SNAP
HA!
Enter the ZyGniC!!!
Don't say it.
Don't say what?
You were going to say, "what's happening?" right?
Ummm...
Zyggy, tell them...
You guys, see this?
That medallion was an energy booster... a battery!
But how?
A Zwullian battery.
It's a long, complicated story.
But right now, we have things to do. What happened here, with the battery...we have cast a stone into the waters of space-time.
As we speak, the ripples...they spread. Soon, the universe shall know... the ZyGniC! has returned!

The universe is not ready for the ZyGniC!...not yet!
We must wind back the clock. Turn back time.
And back to the beginning we go...
This never happened.
Go ZyGniC!!!
snap
Wheeee
eeooOSH!
YEEE!!!
HOW?!

!
Zyggy turned back time. So, here we are...at the beginning.
They are still in their timeline...Scoot doesn't know what happened.
He's still itching for that fight...and nothing I say is going to change his mind...
!!
Well, if that is what he wants...that is what he gets.
Man, know what? This doesn't feel right...we tricked them, after all.
So, what?
But... honestly...
Awww, forget that...what's a riskassion?
DHH
PISKHO
DISHOOM!!
Man, it's spelt R, E, C... Hey! A shooting star!
Bro, that's life for you. Even stars can fall!
What does that even mean?
Nothing. Why does everything have to mean something?
Well...look on the bright side. This can't get any worse, right?
Ummm, usually... it does.

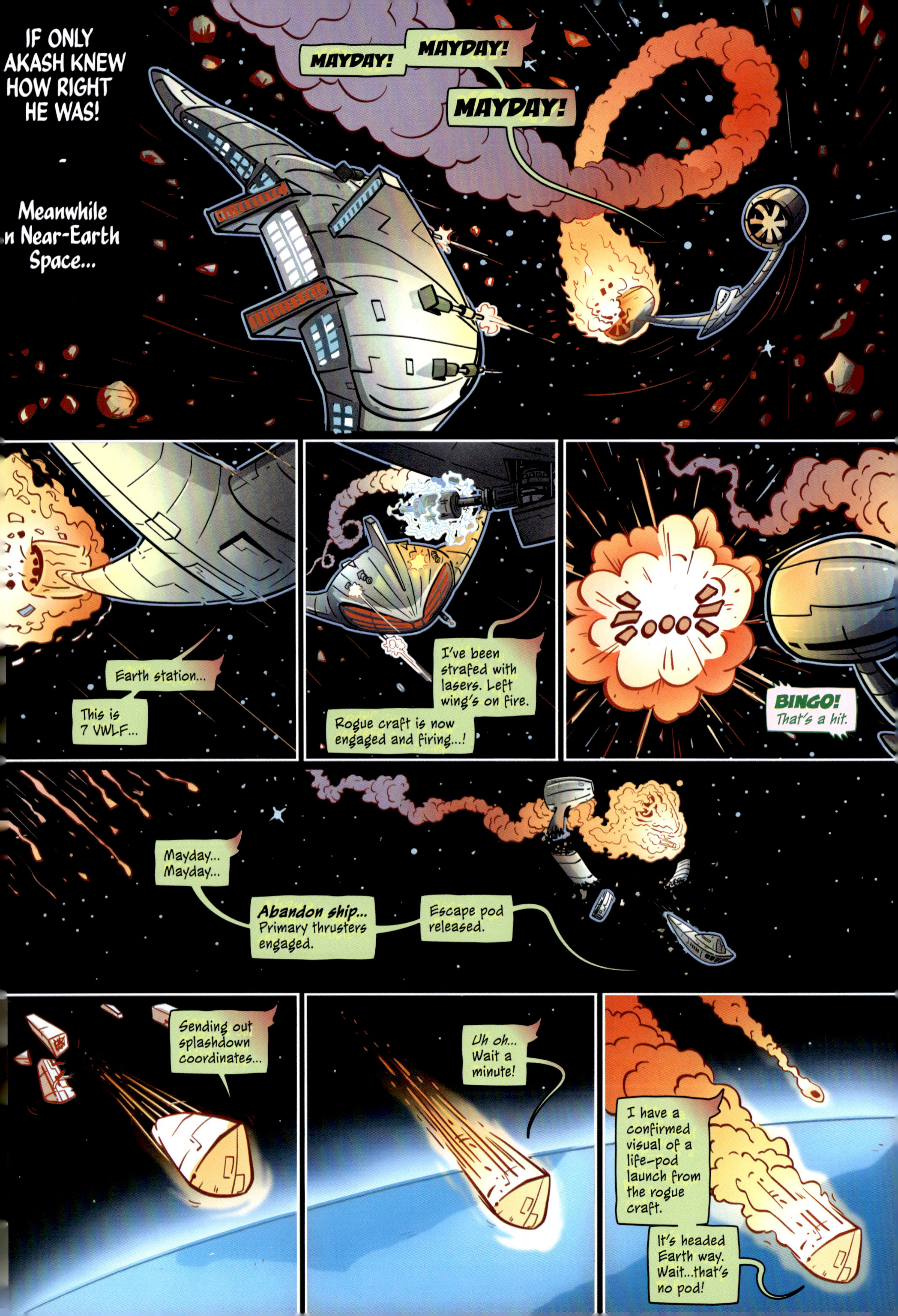
IF ONLY AKASH KNEW HOW RIGHT HE WAS!
-
Meanwhile n Near-Earth Space...
MAYDAY!
MAYDAY!
MAYDAY!
Earth station...
This is 7 VWLF...
I've been strafed with lasers. Left wing's on fire.
Rogue craft is now engaged and firing...!
BINGO! That's a hit.
Mayday... Mayday...
Abandon ship... Primary thrusters engaged.
Escape pod released.
Sending out splashdown coordinates...
Uh oh... Wait a minute!
I have a confirmed visual of a life-pod launch from the rogue craft.
It's headed Earth way. Wait...that's no pod!

A7ZF, Earth control. What is it?
Not sure, probably a war craft. My flotation is compromised. I need a hard landing.
Secondary thrusters active.
Received revised coordinates.
Can you track that craft?
Negative. Forget the craft...activate chutes now!
FWAAAP
Roger. Chutes released and confirmed holding. Landing coordinates set.
Send the rescue team out.
Roger that.
Stop thrusters.
TOUCH DOWN!!!
Hatch opening...
Is that...? No, it couldn't be. Not a Zwullian craft...
What if it is...why now? After all these eons...why here?
SO IT BEGINS...!

COMING SOON!

Aakash and Rehan plan a race. But things go awry, when Scoot and Tic/Toc decide to crash the party! Can Taara save the day...with a *"little"* help from Zyggy?

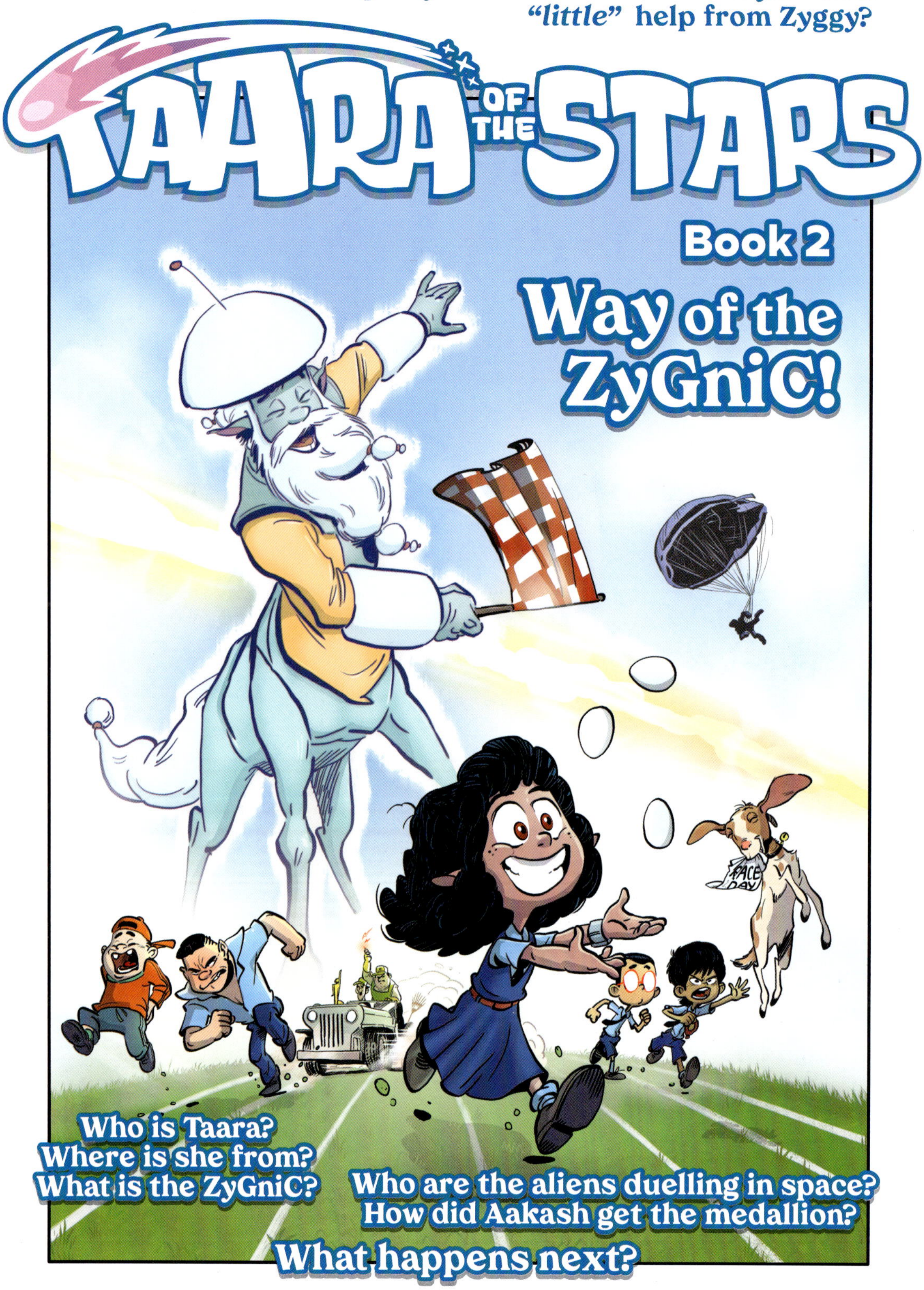

Come explore the vast Zygnian multiverse.
Connect with us at

taaraofthestars.com

Here's a sneak peek into book 2 of the series: ***'Way of the ZyGniC!'***

Remember last time? And what the principal said?
HE HE HE HE HE HE HE HE
There is no excuse for this kind of behaviour. It's *unacceptable!*
THUMP
Shame on you boys, for putting this child at risk!
BUT...BUT...
Shush.
She is not going to be around all the time. Just wait until we catch you alone.
No...no. Please don't!
That was fun. What were they saying?
Umm...nothing!
What did the principal say???
Naaah. No worries. Any more trouble, and he'll **probably** expel you guys.
WHAT???
So, **NO** violence! None at all.
We need to do something, bro. I'm tired of hiding.
Plus, being honest here, we **did** take Scoot's money.
"Borrowed", bro...borrowed.
There must be something we could do to sort all this out.
GUUUYS!
BOINK
EECH!
Did you just...?
What? HEY!!!
NO...Someone just pinged me, that was a tracer signal.
It's the *IGPC*. They are looking for us.
Who?

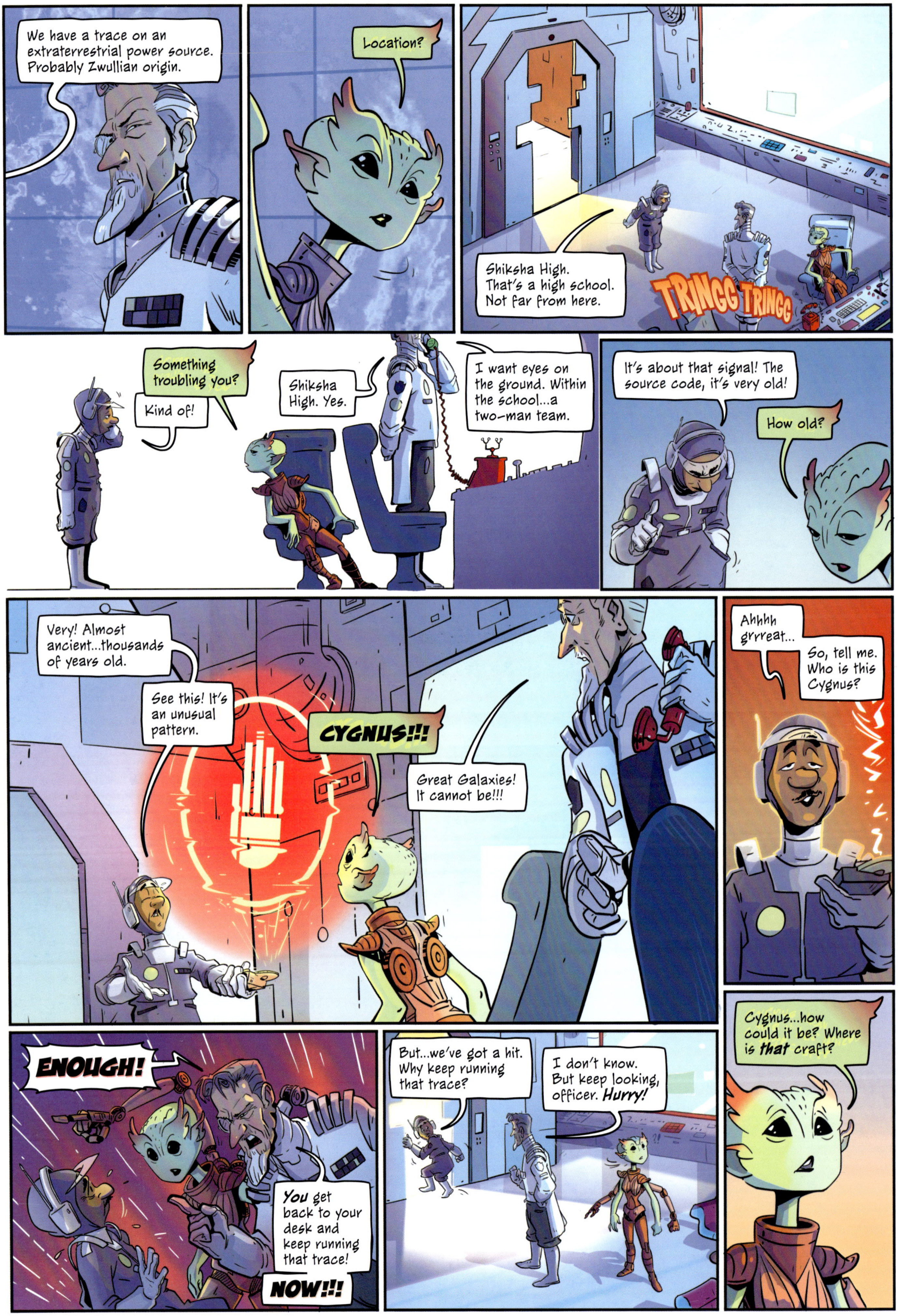
We have a trace on an extraterrestrial power source. Probably Zwullian origin.
Location?
Shiksha High. That's a high school. Not far from here.
TRINGG TRINGG
Something troubling you?
Kind of!
Shiksha High. Yes.
I want eyes on the ground. Within the school...a two-man team.
It's about that signal! The source code, it's very old!
How old?
Very! Almost ancient...thousands of years old.
See this! It's an unusual pattern.
CYGNUS!!!
Great Galaxies! It cannot be!!!
Ahhhh grrreat...
So, tell me. Who is this Cygnus?
ENOUGH!
You get back to your desk and keep running that trace!
NOW!!!
But...we've got a hit. Why keep running that trace?
I don't know. But keep looking, officer. Hurry!
Cygnus...how could it be? Where is that craft?